SNATCHED BY THE DAWN THIEF

DINOSAUR COVE

DINOSAUR COVE™

SNATCHED BY THE DAWN THIEF

by
REX STONE

illustrated by
MIKE SPOOR

Series created by
Working Partners Ltd

OXFORD
UNIVERSITY PRESS

Special thanks to Jan Burchett and Sara Vogler

For Anya, Valda, Stewart and Mum. Live the adventure. R.S.

My illustrations in this book are dedicated to
Maggie, Haydn, and Alessio. M.S.

OXFORD
UNIVERSITY PRESS

Great Clarendon Street, Oxford OX2 6DP
Oxford University Press is a department of the University of Oxford.
It furthers the University's objective of excellence in research, scholarship,
and education by publishing worldwide in

Oxford   New York

Auckland   Cape Town   Dar es Salaam   Hong Kong   Karachi
Kuala Lumpur   Madrid   Melbourne   Mexico City   Nairobi
New Delhi   Shanghai   Taipei   Toronto

With offices in

Argentina   Austria   Brazil   Chile   Czech Republic   France   Greece
Guatemala   Hungary   Italy   Japan   Poland   Portugal   Singapore
South Korea   Switzerland   Thailand   Turkey   Ukraine   Vietnam

Oxford is a registered trade mark of Oxford University Press
in the UK and in certain other countries

Series created by Working Partners Ltd
Dinosaur Cove is a registered trademark of Working Partners Ltd

The moral rights of the author have been asserted

Database right Oxford University Press (maker)

First published 2011

British Library Cataloguing in Publication Data

Data available
ISBN: 978-0-19-278989-1

1 3 5 7 9 10 8 6 4 2

Printed in Great Britain
Paper used in the production of this book is a natural,
recyclable product made from wood grown in sustainable forests
The manufacturing process conforms to the environmental
regulations of the country of origin

FACT FILE

➡️ JAMIE'S DAD'S MUSEUM ON THE BOTTOM FLOOR OF THE LIGHTHOUSE IN DINOSAUR COVE IS THE SECOND BEST PLACE IN THE WORLD TO BE. THE FIRST IS DINO WORLD, OF COURSE, THE SECRET THAT JAMIE AND HIS BEST FRIEND TOM HAVE DISCOVERED IN THE BACK OF A DEEP, DARK CAVE. THEIR TRUSTY DINOSAUR FRIEND, WANNA, COMES ON EVERY ADVENTURE. BUT WHAT IF WANNA STARTS RUNNING WITH THE WRONG CROWD?

JAMIE

- **FULL NAME:** JAMIE MORGAN
- **AGE:** 8 YEARS
- **SIZE:** 1 JATOM*
- **TOP SPEED:** 10 KPH
- **LIKES:** FOSSIL HUNTING AND LEARNING ABOUT DINOSAURS
- **DISLIKES:** BEING STUCK INDOORS

Jamie's eye

Jamie's foot

Jamie's hand

*NOTE: A JATOM IS THE SIZE OF JAMIE OR TOM: 125 CM TALL AND 27 KG IN WEIGHT

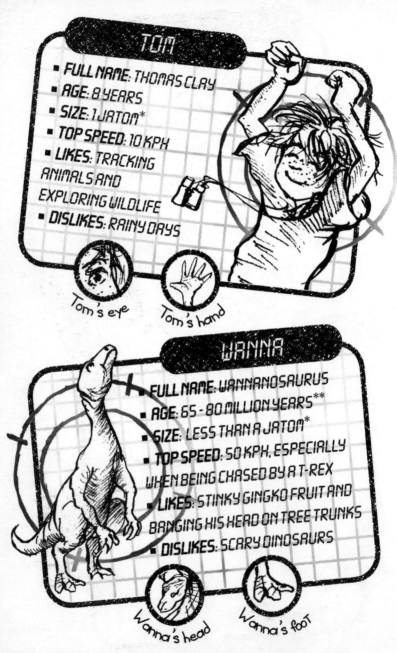

TOM

- FULL NAME: THOMAS CLAY
- AGE: 8 YEARS
- SIZE: 1 JATOM*
- TOP SPEED: 10 KPH
- LIKES: TRACKING ANIMALS AND EXPLORING WILDLIFE
- DISLIKES: RAINY DAYS

Tom's eye

Tom's hand

WANNA

- FULL NAME: WANNANOSAURUS
- AGE: 65 - 80 MILLION YEARS**
- SIZE: LESS THAN A JATOM*
- TOP SPEED: 50 KPH, ESPECIALLY WHEN BEING CHASED BY A T-REX
- LIKES: STINKY GINGKO FRUIT AND BANGING HIS HEAD ON TREE TRUNKS
- DISLIKES: SCARY DINOSAURS

Wanna's head

Wanna's foot

*NOTE: A JATOM IS THE SIZE OF JAMIE OR TOM: 125 CM TALL AND 27 KG IN WEIGHT
**NOTE: SCIENTISTS CALL THIS PERIOD THE LATE CRETACEOUS

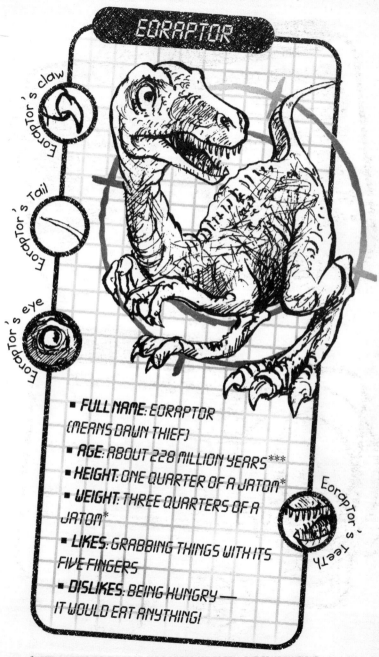

EORAPTOR

Eoraptor's claw

Eoraptor's Tail

Eoraptor's eye

Eoraptor's teeth

- **FULL NAME:** EORAPTOR
(MEANS DAWN THIEF)
- **AGE:** ABOUT 228 MILLION YEARS***
- **HEIGHT:** ONE QUARTER OF A JATOM*
- **WEIGHT:** THREE QUARTERS OF A JATOM*
- **LIKES:** GRABBING THINGS WITH ITS FIVE FINGERS
- **DISLIKES:** BEING HUNGRY — IT WOULD EAT ANYTHING!

*NOTE: A JATOM IS THE SIZE OF JAMIE OR TOM: 125 CM TALL AND 27 KG IN WEIGHT
***NOTE: SCIENTISTS CALL THIS PERIOD THE TRIASSIC

DINOSAUR COVE

Village

Marina

Sealight Head

8

Landslips where clay and fossils are

DINO CAVE

High Tide beach line

Low Tide beach line

Sea

Smuggler's Point

9

CHAPTER 1

Jamie Morgan sat bolt upright in bed. For a moment he couldn't think where he was. There was a strange buzzing in his ear and the walls of his lighthouse bedroom seemed much closer than they should be and he wasn't in his pyjamas. He was fully dressed. Then he remembered. He and his best friend Tom Clay were camping in a tent in his garden—and the buzzing was his portable alarm clock.

He stretched out a hand and pressed the button to silence the alarm.

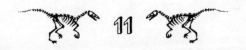

'What time is it?' came Tom's drowsy voice from the sleeping bag next to him.

'Time to get up,' replied Jamie. He crawled to the tent flap and peeped out. The faint light of dawn could just be seen over

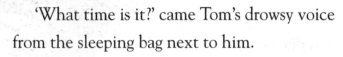

Smuggler's Point and he could already hear a few birds calling.

'It's four in the morning.'

'Too early,' groaned Tom, burrowing further down in his sleeping bag.

Soon Jamie could hear
his muffled snores. He tossed
a pillow at the humped figure.
Tom's bleary face appeared,
tousled hair sticking up in spikes.

'Come on. It was your idea to
camp out so that we could hear
the dawn chorus.'

'Five more minutes,' Tom
complained.

Jamie grinned. 'I could fetch the
hose. Maybe a blast of water will help
you get out of bed?'

'I'm up!' Tom leapt out of his sleeping bag.

They burst through the flap of the tent and
stood on the dewy grass. From the cliffs came
the shrill caws and harsh cries of the seabirds
as they woke and took to the air.

'Some of them sound like they're sawing
wood,' said Tom.

13

'That will be the razorbills,' replied Jamie. 'Grandad said it's like they're having a woodwork class on the cliff.'

Gradually the sky above the cove filled with gulls, calling harshly as they swooped and dived over the sea.

'What a racket!' Tom laughed. 'I can't believe I normally sleep through all this.'

'Got an idea,' shouted Jamie. He lowered his voice. 'What would be even more amazing than hearing the dawn chorus in Dinosaur Cove?'

Tom's face broke into a huge smile. 'Hearing the dawn chorus in Dino World. Awesome!'

Jamie and Tom had a fantastic secret. Deep in the cliffs of Smuggler's

Point they'd discovered the entrance into a wonderful world of living dinosaurs.

'We'll be back before Dad and Grandad are even awake,' said Jamie, slinging his backpack over his shoulder.

'Wait,' said Tom. 'We need an ammonite from your dad's museum or the magic won't work to let us into Dino World.'

Jamie checked his backpack. 'I've got everything in here. Triassic ammonite, Fossil Finder, notebook.'

'And I've got my compass,' said Tom, patting his shorts pocket. 'What are we waiting for?'

The sky was lighter over the headland as the boys scrambled up the rocky cliff to the old smugglers' cave.

Jamie shone his torch into the dark cave, lighting

the way
as they squeezed
into the hidden cave beyond.
His beam lit up the fossilized
footprints in the floor. 'Ready?'
'Ready,' agreed Tom.

Jamie counted as they followed the
footprints to the solid cave wall. 'One, two,
three, four, five...'

Flash!

The smugglers' cave vanished and they stepped out from the hollow tree trunk into the warmth of the Triassic jungle. Pink dawn light flickered through the sparse trees and deafening screeches and roars filled the air.

'This beats the seagulls' noise!' Jamie yelled over the racket. 'It's like listening to a hundred giants with toothache.'

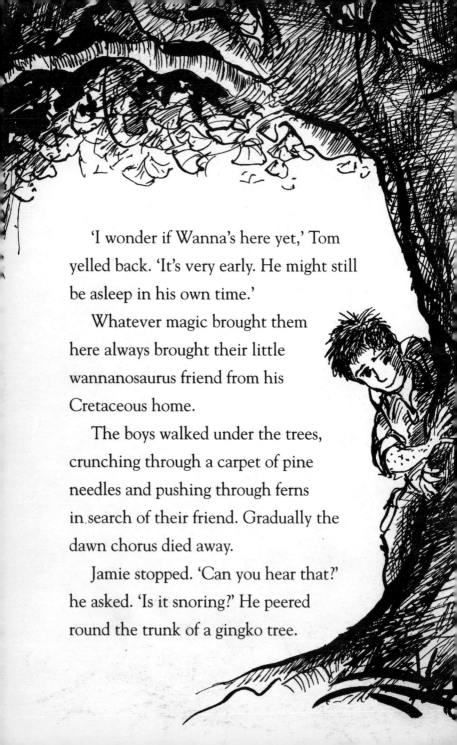

'I wonder if Wanna's here yet,' Tom yelled back. 'It's very early. He might still be asleep in his own time.'

Whatever magic brought them here always brought their little wannanosaurus friend from his Cretaceous home.

The boys walked under the trees, crunching through a carpet of pine needles and pushing through ferns in search of their friend. Gradually the dawn chorus died away.

Jamie stopped. 'Can you hear that?' he asked. 'Is it snoring?' He peered round the trunk of a gingko tree.

'It's Wanna. Fast asleep.'

'Let's leave him for the moment,' suggested Tom. 'I want to get up high so that we can really get a good look at the Triassic sunrise.'

They shinned up the sturdy gingko tree.

'Wow!' gasped Jamie, clinging to the topmost branch. He peered out to where the sun was just beginning to

rise over the hills.
Then he twisted round
towards the desert dunes
in the west. 'Still dark
over there.'

Tom was looking south.
'I've got a fantastic view
of the ocean,' he declared.
'It's ever so calm. I'd love
to see it close up.'

'We could do that today,' suggested Jamie. 'But we can't go without Wanna.'

'He's still asleep,' said Tom. 'Let's wake him up and surprise him.' He picked a handful of gingkoes from the tree, filling his pockets with the bright orange fruit. 'Can't greet him without his favourite stinky snack.'

They climbed down and crept across to their little friend, taking care not to crunch the pine needles beneath their feet. Tom was just reaching out with the gingko when Jamie noticed that Wanna had one eye open and was watching them.

'Look out!' he cried.

It was too late. The little wannanosaurus jumped to his feet and knocked them flying.

Grunking with excitement, Wanna covered their faces with wet raspy licks.

'He was playing a trick on us,' spluttered Tom.

'Hi, boy!' said Jamie, giving Wanna's hard, domed head a welcoming pat. 'Being a Cretaceous dino in the Triassic must seem strange.'

'He doesn't look surprised to be here, though,' said Tom, tossing him the ripe gingkoes. Wanna slurped them up greedily. 'I think he loves our adventures as much as we do.'

The sun had risen higher now, heating
the forest air. Further down the slope a sharp
screeching noise suddenly started up.

'What do you think is making that squawky
racket?' asked Tom, shielding his eyes from the
sunlight flickering through the branches.

'It's coming from the marshy land near the
pond,' said Jamie. 'Let's have a look.'

They pushed through the undergrowth of
horsetail ferns, scattering huge insects with

cobwebby wings as they made
their way towards the marsh.
Wanna ran alongside them,
nose to the ground, looking eager
to be exploring with his friends.
A thin stream wound its way down
towards the muddy ground and
dragonflies as big as blackbirds darted
about over the water.

Tom held up a pretend microphone.
'Three bold Triassic explorers are off on one
of their famous investigations,' he whispered.
'It's early morning in Dino World and, despite
a gentle breeze, it's already hot. Underfoot the
ground is soft and squelchy as they approach
the source of the curious sound. They're
pushing back the cycads and . . . WOW!'

Jamie and Tom stopped dead. In front
of them lay the half-eaten body of a huge
dinosaur, partly submerged in the mud.

A pack of small, skinny creatures was scurrying around it, squabbling with loud scraws as they vied with each other for their meal. The adults were about the size of turkeys and stood on their back legs, digging their long claws into the meat. The little ones scampered round, squealing greedily.

'That's some breakfast!' exclaimed Jamie, running his eyes over the flesh hanging from the ribs of the dead dinosaur. 'It looks familiar.

Wide, croc-like head but with longer legs than a crocodile. And you can just see a few plates left on its back—I reckon it was a postosuchus and I don't think it's been dead long. It looks quite fresh.'

'You're right,' said Tom. 'The question is, what are those funny little things that are eating it?'

Jamie pulled his Fossil Finder from his backpack and turned it on. '*HAPPY HUNTING*' appeared on the screen. He tapped the keys. '*LONG HEAD . . . SHARP TEETH . . . SHORT FRONT LEGS . . . FIVE FINGERS . . .* It says *EORAPTOR, PRONOUNCED EE-OH-RAP-TOR.*' The name means dawn thief.'

'Well, it's dawn, and they're certainly pinching plenty of posto,' Tom said.

27

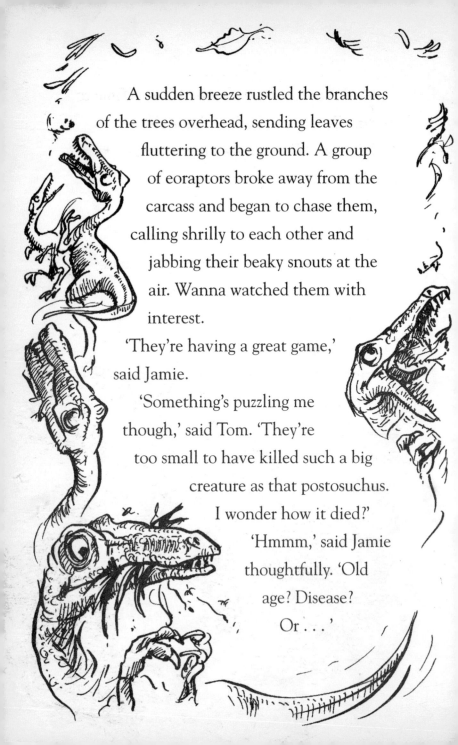

A sudden breeze rustled the branches
of the trees overhead, sending leaves
fluttering to the ground. A group
of eoraptors broke away from the
carcass and began to chase them,
calling shrilly to each other and
jabbing their beaky snouts at the
air. Wanna watched them with
interest.

'They're having a great game,'
said Jamie.

'Something's puzzling me
though,' said Tom. 'They're
too small to have killed such a big
creature as that postosuchus.
I wonder how it died?'

'Hmmm,' said Jamie
thoughtfully. 'Old
age? Disease?
Or . . .'

'Another predator!' finished Tom. 'Time to be dino detectives. Let's look for clues.'

Jamie and Tom stepped out from the trees and began to search around the body.

The soft earth was scattered with the small, birdlike imprints of the ee-ohs.

'Check these out!' called Tom, pointing to some large indents in the boggy ground.

'Footprints,' said Jamie, looking at the mass of churned-up mud. 'And they're huge. Is this our killer?'

Before the boys could investigate, they heard a scraping sound nearby. They looked up to see Wanna pawing the ground.

'I know what he's up to,' said Jamie. 'He's going to show his new friends his special way of getting food.'

The ee-ohs pressed round him, nudging him with their snouts and squawking excitedly.

Grunk!

The little wannanosaurus backed away from the pack, put his head down, and

charged full pelt at the
trunk of a tall cycad tree.

WHAM!

The tree shuddered as his
bony head slammed into it and
seeds showered down all over the
watching ee-ohs. Wanna and the
ee-ohs licked up the seeds. The
meal was soon over and the ee-ohs
gathered round him again.

'They look in awe of him,'
laughed Jamie.

WHAM!

'He's like a god,'
said Tom. 'He made
food fall from the
sky, after all.'

Wanna aimed
at another tree.

'He's not going
to roam far while he's
got such a good audience,'
said Jamie. 'Let's go on
investigating these prints.' He stared
at the massive indents in the ground.
'I wonder what made them.'

'Whatever it was, I hope it's not still
around,' exclaimed Tom. 'The prints aren't
very clear but one thing's for sure—whatever
they came from must be huge.'

'There's more over here,' said Jamie,
squelching through the mud. 'Hey! I've found
a really good one.'

Tom came to join him and they studied
the print.

'It's made a deep dent so it's big and heavy,
just as I thought,' said Tom. 'There's five claws
and . . . ' He looked back at the body of the
posto. 'We're so dumb. These are postosuchus
footprints. The posto made these itself!'

Jamie measured
the massive indent
with his hands
and compared
it with the foot
of the dead
reptile. 'Wait a
minute,' he said.
'Our posto's
much smaller
than the one
that made
those.'

'You're right,' exclaimed Tom. He peered at the line of prints. 'And these are facing away from the body. Then there's only one explanation. It was killed by a much bigger posto.' He pointed along the line of prints that led away into the distance. 'And that one went off that way.'

'They probably had a fight for territory,' said Jamie. 'Well, I'm glad the victor's gone. We wouldn't want to meet it.'

'Too right,' said Tom. 'Let's not hang around here. Time to head for the ocean.'

'Agreed,' said Jamie eagerly. 'Come on, Wanna. Wanna?'

There was no answering grunk.

The little wannanosaurus was bounding
happily away through the trees with his new
ee-oh friends.

'Wanna!' yelled Jamie. He looked
worried. 'This isn't his world. He could
get lost and never find his way back
to his own time.
We have to go
after him.'

Crunching over
the dry pine
needles of the forest
floor they chased
after Wanna and
the pack.

'It's all right for them,' panted Tom as they dodged round ferns and wove between the conifers after the chattering ee-ohs. 'But we're not so fast in Triassic forests.'

The boys burst out of the trees and into the dry heat of the scrubland. They ran for what seemed like miles, their trainers churning up dust as they went. When they finally reached the fertile river, Wanna and the ee-ohs splashed right across and swarmed onwards up a hill on the other side.

Jamie and Tom followed them across the shallow riverbed and made for the hill. At the top they skidded to a halt, gasping in the hot air. An amazing view stretched out in front of

them. The hill sloped down for some distance
until it stopped suddenly at a jagged cliff edge.
And beyond lay the calm blue sea, sparkling
in the early morning sunshine.

A burst of grunking and chattering broke
out from down the hill.

'I recognize that racket.' Jamie grinned.

Wanna and the younger eoraptors were
scampering about among the rocks and trees
at the edge of the cliff. The older ones were

sitting in a nearby
nest made of
branches and leaves.

'I reckon they're
playing prehistoric
hide-and-seek!'
declared Tom. 'Let's
leave him and get down to the sea.
I'd love a paddle in the Triassic ocean.'

But Jamie was staring out over the
distant water.

'What's that splash of light on the
horizon?' he exclaimed. 'It looks like a bright
orange sun, but that's impossible. We can see
the real one in the east.'

'I know we've come across some amazing
stuff here in Dino World,' said Tom, puzzled,
'but there have never been two suns. What
can it be?'

'A new scientific discovery?' said Jamie.

'Awesome!' said Tom. 'Let's check it out.' Suddenly he clutched Jamie's arm. 'Whoa! What's that?'

'The ground's moving,' cried Jamie. 'It's an earthquake!'

Wanna and the ee-ohs stopped their game and looked around, puzzled. Then they carried on playing.

'It's only a small one,' said Tom as he felt little shudders run through his trainers and up his legs. 'It hasn't stopped the dino game.'

'Never been in a real earthquake before,' said Jamie, listening to the faint

underground
rumblings.

'It's cool!'

But now stones
and rubble were
jumping around
their feet and the
ground was shaking
more violently.
Wanna and his
friends gave
frightened squawks.

Tom saw a
crack snaking
towards Jamie's feet.

'Watch out!' he shouted.

But it was too late. In a second his
friend had disappeared into the
crumbling earth.

CHAPTER 4

Horrified, Tom flattened himself on the ground and edged towards where Jamie had disappeared.

He peered fearfully into the crack in the earth. To his enormous relief, he saw that Jamie hadn't fallen far. He was wedged in the gap a little way down.

'You all right?' he gasped.

'Think so,' called Jamie. He managed a wobbly grin. 'Just stuck! Can you give me a hand up?'

Tom reached out to Jamie. Their fingers touched and missed. Tom wriggled further forwards, sending a shower of earth over Jamie's head.

'Sorry!' he called, as his friend spluttered and choked.

He reached down again, grasped Jamie firmly by the wrist and pulled with all his strength.

Scraping his elbows and knees on the rough rock, Jamie struggled out, brushing dust from his hair.

'Thanks,' he said. 'Maybe earthquakes aren't as cool as I thought.' He jumped up. 'Let's make sure Wanna's OK.'

They set off down the hill, and over the rocky, cracked ground to the cliff edge. The ee-ohs were swarming around a clump of stacked branches and pine needles under the trees.

'His friends are there,' said Tom. 'And I think that's their nest. The babies are in the middle. But where's Wanna?' He sounded worried.

A hard, domed head popped up amongst the young ee-ohs.

'There he is!' Jamie laughed. 'He's having a second breakfast.'

The adult dinos were scampering to and fro with gingkoes and cycad seeds for their important guest.

'He won't be going anywhere while the ee-ohs are making such a fuss of him,' said

Jamie. 'We've got time to check out that strange sun.'

'Let's get down on the beach,' answered Tom eagerly. 'We've got an important discovery to make.'

Jamie headed along the cliff, looking for a way to the beach. He stepped on to a small ledge just below the cliff edge. 'There's another shelf further down,' he called. 'It's a sort of zigzag path.'

Tom nodded. 'I reckon it's been made by dinosaurs finding their way to the sea just like us.'

They followed slippery ledges and grooves all the way down the cliff, grabbing at plants and rough edges for handholds. At last they reached the gritty black sand of the beach.

In front of them lay a vast, craggy bay, the sea lapping gently at the sand.

'Hey, check out those rocks way over there,' said Jamie, shading his eyes. 'They look like the back of a steggie.'

He walked to the water's edge, where the waves lapped at his shoes. Tom joined him and together they scanned the horizon. Far out to sea, the orange ball glowed brightly.

'What on earth can it be?' asked Jamie.

'I don't know,' said Tom. 'But I think it's getting bigger.'

'You're right!' said Jamie. 'This is so weird.'

Then they both felt it. A shivering in the soft sand beneath them.

'It's another tremor,' shouted Tom. He reached for his binoculars and focused on the strange ball of fire. 'Wow! There's black smoke . . . and sparks . . . and spurting lava. That's not a second sun. It's a volcano—and it's erupting.'

He thrust the binoculars into Jamie's hand. Out to sea Jamie could see a small rocky island. The smoke and flames were belching from it, rising high into the sky.

'Awesome!' exclaimed Jamie.

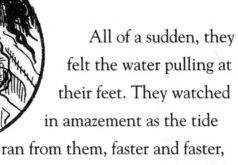

All of a sudden, they felt the water pulling at their feet. They watched in amazement as the tide ran from them, faster and faster, making a weird sucking noise as it went.

'That's odd,' called Tom. He inspected the seabed, rapidly drying out in the hot sunshine. 'But look at the view we're getting of underwater life.' He bent down to inspect some green algae that flopped on the sand. 'Hey! There's an ammonite—a live one.'

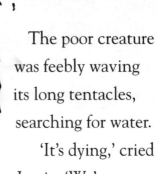

The poor creature
was feebly waving
its long tentacles,
searching for water.

'It's dying,' cried
Jamie. 'We've got
to get it to the sea.'

Then he realized that
the tide was still going out,
sucking at the rocks and seaweed. 'But it's
too far away.'

'Something's wrong,' Tom said.

Jamie turned to face him. 'When tides go
out really quickly like this, it can only mean
one thing,' he said urgently. 'There's a giant
wave coming—you know—a tsunami! Run!'

They sprinted for the cliff and leapt up the
path, their feet slipping in their haste to reach
the top.

'Got to get as high as possible,' panted Tom.

Jamie looked out to sea. He could see a wave clearly now against the sky—a solid wall of water moving across the sea towards them.

CHAPTER 5

SEARCH:

Slipping and sliding, the boys scrambled up the jagged path. It was hard to catch their breath in the thin Triassic air, and loose earth and stones fell away as they climbed.

Behind them, the tsunami was rolling relentlessly closer, growing bigger and bigger.

'Keep going!' puffed Tom as he stretched desperately for the next handhold.

At last they hauled themselves on to the top of the cliff and gazed back in horror at the roaring wall of water.

'The wave's already reached the steggie rocks,' gasped Jamie. The row of pointed rocks vanished as the tsunami swallowed them up.

Tom looked round. 'Where's Wanna? He's not in the nest. We need to get him away from here, and save the ee-ohs too. They could be swept away.'

'There he is,' said Jamie, pointing to where their dino friend was play-fighting on the cliff edge with a group of young eoraptors. The larger ee-ohs suddenly stiffened and sniffed the air. They began to chatter among themselves and squeal in alarm.

A second later they'd gone, scampering away towards the safety of the hill. Now just Wanna and his little playmates were left.

'The older ones can sense the danger,' said Tom anxiously, 'but Wanna and the babies are too busy with their game.'

'Here, Wanna,' shouted Jamie. 'If he comes, perhaps the young ee-ohs will follow. Wanna!' But their dino friend took no notice.

The boys could hear the deep, threatening rumble of the huge wave as it rolled towards the cliff. Wanna stopped playing and stiffened.

'He's picked up the sound!' cried Tom.

'Come on, boy!' called Jamie. 'We have to get to higher ground.' He turned to Tom, his eyes wide with fear. 'That wave might not be as tall as the cliff now but tsunamis grow taller as they get into shallower water. It could swamp us all!'

Grunk! Grunk!

Wanna scampered up to Jamie and Tom and butted them anxiously with his head.

'That's the idea, Wanna,' said Tom. 'But
we can't go yet. We have to make sure your
little friends come too.' He tried to shoo the
ee-ohs but they just thought it was all part of
their game and ran nearer the cliff edge.

The noise of the wave was thunderous
now. Tom could see its crest, rising to
an enormous height as it approached.

'The wave's three times as tall
as your grandad's lighthouse now!'
'Got an idea,' exclaimed Jamie.
'Remember how the ee-ohs played with
the leaves? We can distract them with
something.' He grabbed his torch and
shone the beam over the ground near
them, but the ee-ohs took no notice.
'The torchlight's not bright enough,'
he cried in despair.

'I've got it,' yelled Tom. He took his
compass and caught the early sun on it, making
the bright reflection dance over the ground.
Two of the young ee-ohs stopped their play and
watched, their heads on one side.

'It's working!' muttered Jamie. He held
up the shiny screen of the Fossil Finder to
the sun and aimed the light so that it danced
around Tom's flickering beam. The young
eoraptors ran over, chasing the curious

movement. And now their friends saw what they were doing and came to join the fun.

'The wave's going to hit any second!' yelled Tom. 'Let's get them out of here!'

They dashed up the hill, making the lights dance across the hard ground behind them. Wanna and the little dinos followed, chattering eagerly.

'They think it's a game!' shouted Jamie over the tremendous roar of the tsunami.

He glanced over his shoulder as he ran, and saw the towering wave bearing down on the cliff.

CRASH!

The wall of water hit the cliff top, sending huge shock waves through the ground.

CHAPTER 6

Fountains of spray rose high in the air, soaking the boys and the little dinos in seconds. Wanna shook himself like a dog.

'We made it,' cried Tom, wiping the salt water from his eyes. 'And we saved the little ee-ohs!'

At that moment there was a thunderous crash. Jamie whipped round and his heart nearly stopped.

'We're not safe yet,' he yelled. 'The cliff's breaking away!'

Jamie and Tom saw with horror that the
cliff top was sliding away as if the sea was
trying to gobble it up.

'The power of the water's too much for the
cliff,' yelled Jamie. 'It's going to be destroyed.
We need to get even higher.'

Tom looked out to sea.
'There's another wave
coming—and it's bigger than
the first one!'

The terrified baby
ee-ohs were scampering
ahead up the hill. Wanna
started after them, then ran
back to the boys.

Grunk! Grunk, Grunk!
'We're coming,
Wanna,' cried Jamie.
The boys raced for their lives after
their little friend. Right behind

them great swathes of land were
tumbling into the sea.

The next crash of water sent
waves foaming round their feet.
Wanna gave a grunk of alarm but
kept on running.

Breathless, they reached the
top of the hill. The ee-ohs hadn't
stopped. They were bolting across the
scrubland, making for the marsh.

'Are we safe?' panted Tom, bent
double, trying to fill his lungs.

Jamie looked back. The gentle
slope of the hill they had just
climbed was gone. They were
on the edge of a huge drop.
Far below the water was
being sucked back towards
an unbelievably huge
wall of water.

'NO!' he shrieked.

They launched themselves down the hill,
desperately running towards the distant forest.

CRASH!

Everything shook beneath their feet as
the wave hit the hill like an explosion. Rivers
of water came rushing towards them
and they stumbled and splashed
through the rising currents,
fighting to keep their footing.
The dry, dusty earth had
turned to mud, clinging to
their trainers.

'I can't run any more,'
gasped Jamie. 'The ground's
too squelchy. If another
wave hits we'll be
washed away in
the flood.'

Tom glanced nervously over his shoulder. The water was slowly draining away, leaving lakes and puddles all over the flat scrubland. 'It's OK,' he said with a sigh of relief. 'Hear how quiet it is now? There are no more.'

They waded through the shallow pools of water to reach the first of the forest trees.

'This land's never going to be the same again,' said Jamie. 'The hill and cliffs have gone.'

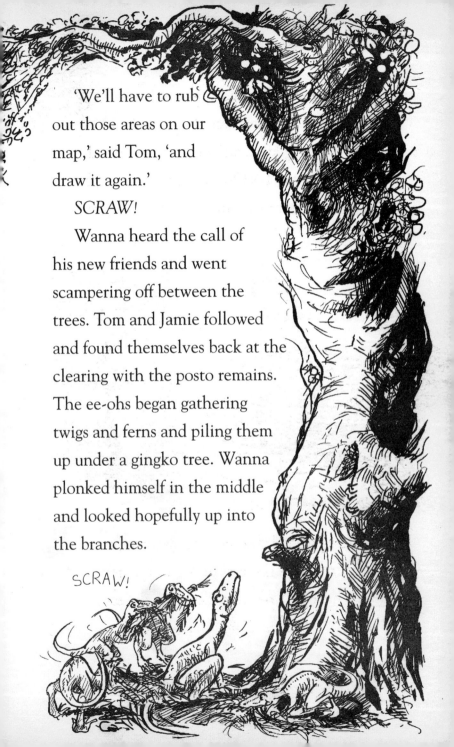

'We'll have to rub
out those areas on our
map,' said Tom, 'and
draw it again.'

SCRAW!

Wanna heard the call of
his new friends and went
scampering off between the
trees. Tom and Jamie followed
and found themselves back at the
clearing with the posto remains.
The ee-ohs began gathering
twigs and ferns and piling them
up under a gingko tree. Wanna
plonked himself in the middle
and looked hopefully up into
the branches.

SCRAW!

'They're building a new nest,' said Tom.
'Sensible place this time. No huge waves—
and plenty of posto takeaway.'

'Talking of takeaways,' said Jamie, licking
his lips. 'It's time for one of Grandad's
breakfasts.'

'Is he doing his special eggy bread?' said
Tom eagerly.

Jamie nodded. 'He promised he would.'

'Race you back to the hollow tree then.'

Wanna scampering happily along at their
heels, the boys darted through the forest to
the rotting tree trunk that would lead them
back to their own time. They gave their little
dino friend a goodbye
pat and picked him
one more gingko.

Wanna grunked happily with
his mouth full of the stinky fruit,
then turned and trotted into the
hollow tree and disappeared.

'He's off back to the Cretaceous,'
said Tom. 'I wonder where we'll meet
him next?'

'It's time for us to get home too,'
said Jamie.

Putting their feet into the
dino prints, they walked
backwards and

soon found themselves in the cold smugglers'
cave.

Outside, the early morning sun was already
warming Dinosaur Cove. The boys made it to
the tent just as Grandad appeared at the door
of the lighthouse, two steaming mugs in his
hands.

'Hot chocolate for the
bird watchers,' he called.
'And breakfast is nearly
ready. How was your dawn
adventure? Was it as good
as you hoped?'

The boys grinned
at each other. If only
Grandad knew what dawn
adventure they'd really had.

'It was the best ever!'
declared Jamie.

DINOSAUR WORLD

---- BOYS' ROUTE

Desert

Fertile river

Oasis

Ocean

76

Can you
discover my secret?